AF490350

ADDICTION
FREE

NR28
production

ADDICTION FREE

ADDICTION FREE

by

Mike Ash

CONTENTS

INTRODUCTION

There I was, reminiscing on my new year's agenda and sincerely hoping to be free from my self drought. Lust had eaten me up because of a single mistake, I wished I was wise enough to run away from the very on set.

I had tried countless times to stop it but I couldn't, I was lost, addicted to everything sex and sensuality. I went online, watched videos, read books and researched on how to break free, but the best I got was to confide in others which was such a bideal. How do i even begin telling people what I was so ashamed of? part of my research even suggested that it was normal but I knew there was more, I had grown into self resentment as I felt compelled time after time to unleash my personal desires anyhow, anywhere. It kept getting worst and the more I tried, the deeper I found myself in it, until I found out I was bound by the spirit of addiction.

WHAT IS ADDITION?

An addiction is a chronic dysfunction of the brain system that involves reward, motivation, and memory. It's about the way your body craves a substance or behavior, especially if it causes a compulsive or obsessive pursuit of "reward" and lack of concern over consequences. Or Addiction is habit or practice that damages, jeopardizes or shortens one's life but when ceased causes trauma. it can also be seen as a pathological relationship to mood altering experience that has life damaging consequences.

It causes trauma when you try to run off and so you have to stick to it or suffer withdrawal symptoms.

In our societies today, when people hear of addiction their mind moves straight to drugs, alcohol and other relating to substance intake. But there are other forms of addiction that we have neglected such as sexual addiction (sex, pornography, Masturbation etc). They all have psychological effects and may even be worst than drugs because it can easily go unnoticed and during that point of self hatred can lead to violence, rape, or even suicide.

MY STORY

It all started when I got a VR case for phones and my friends were like, "imagine watching pornography with this thing, no one would even notice". Although it was just an idea, I decided to give it a try and it was crazy. Everything zoomed to your personal space and stuffs, it felt like I was there with them and soon after it became a daily routine. I would

always tell myself, it's just for fun,
I'm not hooked, I can stop
whenever.

And so from Just watching, I
slipped into the worst kind of self
sex ever, I never fully understood
what I we doing until it to daily
uncontrollable masturbation. At first,
it was all enjoyable but then I felt
empty because I was never satisfied,
I went from regular pornography to
choking and BDSM even to lesbian
pornography, but I was still empty, I
was never OK. I would normally

masturbate 2 to 5 times a night, I spent all my data on porn sites, or checking out porn stars. It was my deep dark secret and I felt really ashamed about myself for that.

Day after day I would sit thinking of how to get of, but the more I tried, the deeper I fell into it. I felt worthless, dirty and started becoming violent. I was mostly isolated and I had to struggle with pretending as if all is well when it felt like I was dying inside. day after day, week after week the emptiness grew until I started into female weight lifters porn, even animation porn. I was personally wrecked, I would take bathroom breaks at work to watch porn and masturbate. All this kept killing me inside, little by little I lost friends, I couldn't concentrate and it just felt like I was drowning and couldn't get help.

I took time searching the internet, looking for help, for an escape route but found none. I kept regretting why I ever started, why I even thought of trying it out. Weeks became months and months became years. During the end of the year I would make a resolution that I won't repeat the mistake in the new year but I would still regress even deeper after a couple of days. it was so uncomfortable taking bathroom breaks just to watch porn and masturbate, I had issues being around female because I became afraid that I might rape them, at some point my choice became going to hookers for sex.

Amidst all this, I never knew there was an easy solution to my problem. A place where I never checked and if had to be a bold step to humility. A lot of people may think it has to do with mindset and decisions, of course I agree, but there's more to that. it took humility, love and discipline to break free. I was tired of my life, I felt there was no more hope and I constantly felt dirty apart from the fact that I had to wash off after every round of annoying self sex session. There was a time I learnt how to make a tool called pocket pussy, it's like a vibrator but for men.

Time after time I cannot count how many times I invented things to satisfy my lust. But today I can boldly say "I AM FREE" all thanks to God.

Now you might be wondering what does God have to do with breaking free from addiction, and my answer is "EVERYTHING". It took understanding God in humility to break free from years of personal torment. I took the bold step, went out for alter call and made the decision to stick to God and it has worked out amazingly.

EFFECTS/DANGERS OF ADDICTION

What addiction really does is to disconnect you from purpose, isolate you into a small space of self denial and self hatred. Addiction puts you into an island of regrets and invites thoughts that can be very harmful to your mental and physical personality.

Although different forms of addiction comes with different symptoms and threats, where the danger begins is denying that you're addicted. sometimes you might not even know until you're faced with a situation that chokes you. their effects includes anxiety or depression, increased isolation, decreased physical activity, low self-esteem, and poor work or school performance, among many others.

FREE THROUGH CHRIST

after taking that bold step to Christ at the alter knowing well that it's not my first time, in fact I had gone countless times but it didn't make sense until this special day, the church was going on a 21days fast which I joined and after that, everything changed.

I am going to let you in on a secret. it's not just about saying you surrender to Christ or about fasting, it's more about the knowledge.Remember I said it takes humility, decisions and consistency to break free.

I was humble enough to be taught the importance and power of fasting and praying. Isaiah 58: 6 says;

Is not this the fast that I have chosen? to loose the bands of wickedness, to undo the heavy burdens, and to let the oppressed go free, and that ye break every yoke?

With this I understood that the

oppressed will go free, yokes will break and everything restored if we ask God sincerely. I was also made to understand that fasting tortures the flesh so the spirit can gain more control of the body. imagine depriving your body of its basic need. if you can stay

without food, then you can stay without that thing that is holding you bound. In my case, I always felt really hungry after masturbation and I will regularly remind myself that if I try it, I might faint because there won't be food at the moment. It wasn't an easy task, but with dedication, persistence and humility I conquered and you can too.

CONCLUSION

We have a lot of untold cases of addiction in different tiers of our lives. This are rarely noticed because humans have a way of hiding things, sometimes we go through a lot without having the courage to share our conditions or situations with people who might be able to help us mostly because of trust issues or privacy. sometimes we think we can endure it a little while longer, but longer we stay, the deeper we get entangled in our mess.

from my story, I had to keep my issues to myself without being able to share them even with the people closest to me because at first I felt I could handle it and then secondly because of pride. I didn't want people to find out I was such a mess.   But I found solace through Christ and I really wish we all do.

Though some addictions are harder to get out from than others, I still think they work with the same principles. Hence, if you can deny yourself food, go to Christ with a broken heart and ask for help and most importantly stay consistent, we can break through anything for with Christ, all things are possible